Dolls & Fairies

Series Editor: Lesley Sims
Reading Consultant: Alison Kelly
Roehampton University

Contents

Page 3
Stories of
Dolls

Page 49
Stories of
Fairies

Stories
of
Dolls

Susanna Davidson

Illustrated by
Amandine Wanert

Designed by Hannah Ahmed

Contents

Chapter 1
The doll's house   3

Chapter 2
The singing doll   17

Chapter 3
The lost doll   35

The doll's house

Amy and Tina loved Cherry
Tree Cottage. "It's the prettiest
doll's house ever," said Tina.

"And Molly's the best doll's owner," Amy added. "We're so lucky to live here."

"You may feel lucky," said Cordelia. "I *don't*!" Cordelia was a beautiful doll and she knew it.

She had golden curls tied up with a shiny clip and a dress that sparkled with sequins.

"I don't belong here," said Cordelia, "I should be in a doll's *palace*. Not stuck in this stuffy, boring cottage."

"It's boring because you never *do* anything," said Amy. "You never help clean or tidy."

"I have more important things to do," snapped Cordelia. "Like brushing my hair."

"Please stop fighting," said Tina. And they had to, as just then they heard Molly.

The dolls rushed back to where Molly had left them and stayed as still as they could.

"It's a sunny day," Molly told them, "so I'm taking you all on a picnic." She carefully picked up the dolls and put them in her basket.

"Oh dear," sighed Cordelia, as Molly set them down on an old rug. "I hope my dress doesn't get dirty."

8

"Look at your sequins and your clip," Tina whispered, to cheer her up. "They're sparkling in the sun."

But far above in the sky, a magpie had spotted Cordelia too. Like all magpies, he loved collecting sparkly things.

At last they came to a tall tree. The magpie dropped Cordelia into his spiky nest.

"Take me back this second," ordered Cordelia.

The magpie shook his head. "You're mine now," he said, then flew away on his bright, glossy wings.

"Oh!" cried Cordelia. "This is horrible." She spent all day in the nest, feeling lonelier and lonelier.

I'm ruined.

"Please help me," she called to a passing magpie.

"Only if you give me your shiny clip," said the magpie.

12

"I'll give you anything you want," sobbed Cordelia. "Just take me home."

At Cherry Tree Cottage, Molly was putting Amy and Tina to bed. "I'll never see Cordelia again," she thought, sadly.

13

Suddenly, there was a shout. "Molly!" called her mother. "Look who I found by the back door."

There, in the palm of her hand, sat Cordelia. Her curls were ragged and wild and her dress was dirty and torn.

14

"Cordelia!" cried Molly, carefully tucking her into bed. "I can't believe you're back."

"Nor can I," said Amy, once Molly had left. "I thought you hated Cherry Tree Cottage."

15

"It's no palace," Cordelia said, "but it's *much* better than a bird's nest. Anyway," she added sadly, "I've lost my sparkle now."

"Never mind," said Amy. "At least you won't be stolen by a magpie again."

16

Chapter 2

The singing doll

Emily had *always* been Kate's best doll. Kate played with her every day and took her to bed each night.

17

"And now," Emily told the other toys proudly, "I'm going to the hospital with her."

It's an important job.

"Why is Kate going to the hospital?" asked Teddy.

"She's having her tonsils taken out," said Emily.

18

"It's not serious," Emily went on. "But she'll need *me* to take care of her."

Next morning, Kate packed her bag. She was going to the hospital that afternoon.

19

Kate sat nervously on her bed, hugging Emily. "Don't worry," Emily told her silently. "I'll be with you."

The door opened and Kate's parents came in. "We've bought you something," said her dad, handing her a present.

20

"A new doll!" cried Kate.
"And look," said her mother,
"she walks and sings."

Kate ran out of the room,
clutching her new doll. "I'm
going to show her to all my
friends," she said, excitedly.

When Kate came back, she didn't even look at her other toys. She carefully placed the new doll next to her bag and went downstairs.

The other toys crowded around the new doll. "What's your name?" asked Teddy.

"Florinda," she said, with a flick of her long, silky hair.

"Why are you sitting by Kate's bag?" asked Emily. She suddenly had an awful feeling.

"*I'm* going to the hospital with Kate," said Florinda. All the toys gasped.

23

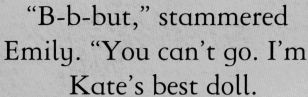

"B-b-but," stammered Emily. "You can't go. I'm Kate's best doll. I go everywhere with her."

I always have.

"Not any more," said Florinda, standing up. "Kate doesn't want you now. You can't talk *or* sing."

"Yes I can!" Emily insisted.
"But not when she's there.
Look!" said Florinda, pressing
a button on
her tummy.

The next moment a small
CD inside her started to play,
"Mary, Mary, quite contrary,
how does your garden grow?"

25

"Wow!" said Teddy, impressed.

"Teddy!" said Emily.

"Sorry," said Teddy.

"And that's not all," Florinda added. "If I press this button, I can talk to Emily." And she pressed another button.

26

"Hello, I'm Florinda," said a
tinny voice.
"What else can you do?"
asked Teddy.

Watch!

Florinda pressed a third
button. Her legs flew up into
the air and she started
marching around the room.

27

"No wonder Kate prefers Florinda," Emily said, glumly. "Ha!" said Florinda. "You don't stand a chance."

"Can you do everything at the same time?" asked Teddy.

"Of course I can!" cried Florinda, pressing every button on her body.

Soon she was marching, talking and singing all at once. "Hello, I'm Mary, Mary, how does your Florinda grow?"

"Stop! Stop!" cried Emily. "I can hear footsteps."

Florinda frantically pressed all her buttons. She stopped talking and walking. But she couldn't stop singing. "How does your garden grow, grow, grow..." sang the tinny voice.

30

"How strange," said Kate's
mother, coming into the room.
"The doll's turned herself on."
"And she won't stop!" said
Kate's dad, covering his ears.
"Turn her off!"

31

"I can't," said Kate's mother, pressing the button again and again.

"Grow, grow, grow, grow..." sang Florinda.

"Please fix her," said Kate. "We've got to leave now and I really want to take her."

"Grow, grow, grow, grow..." sang Florinda.

"There's no time," said Kate's mother. "You'll just have to take another toy."

Kate looked around her room. "I'll take Emily," she said, picking her up and hugging her. "She might not be new, but she's still my best doll."

Chapter 3

The lost doll

It was the day of the school
fair. Daisy ran from table to
table, her rag doll, Ella,
bumping behind her.

The toy table was the best. Daisy propped up Ella, so she could see too.

Look!

"There you are!" said Daisy's mother. "I've been searching for you everywhere. It's time to go home."

She took Daisy's hand and led her to the car. But Daisy had forgotten something...

"I'd like that doll," said a tall man, pointing to Ella.
"No!" thought Ella. "I'm Daisy's." But there was nothing she could do.

Later that evening, the man
showed Ella to his daughter.
"Look, Sophie!" he said.
"I've bought you a
new doll."

"But I've got Mia," Sophie
replied, holding up her rag doll.
Her dad's face fell.
"But thank you," Sophie
went on, taking Ella.

That night, as Sophie slept,
Ella lay awake in the dark,
crying silent doll tears.

"What's the matter?" asked
Berry, a large brown bear.

"I miss my owner, Daisy. She
left me at the school fair by
mistake. I don't belong here."

"Don't worry," said Mia.
"We'll help you find Daisy."
"Th-th-thank you,"
sniffed Ella. "But how?"

"I've got an idea," said Berry.
"Sophie must go to the same
school as Daisy. If Ella gets
into Sophie's school bag..."

"...she can go to school and find Daisy," finished Mia. "Brilliant, Berry! Let's put the plan into action tomorrow, when Sophie's at breakfast."

But the next morning, there was a small problem...

SOPHIE

"I'll never reach the bag," sighed Ella. "It's too high." "We'll help!" came a cry from the top shelf. The next moment, a line of tiny monkeys came tumbling down.

"Climb aboard, Ella," cried the nearest monkey.

42

Ella climbed up the monkey chain. Soon, she could almost reach the bag. Then the bedroom door started to open...

"Jump!" cried the monkeys. Ella jumped. Just in time.

43

As Sophie ran to catch the school bus, she never guessed who she was taking with her.

SOPHIE

At school, Sophie dumped her bag in the classroom and rushed off to assembly.

Ella peered out and gasped. The room was huge. "How will I ever find Daisy?" she wondered.

45

And then, at
the other end of
the classroom,
she spotted
Daisy's bag.

When Daisy got home,
she couldn't believe her eyes.
"Look!" she cried, "Ella's come
back to me."

Meanwhile, Sophie couldn't find her new doll anywhere.

"I don't mind," she told her dad, "I only need one doll. But look at the note I found in my bag. I don't understand it..."

Dear Mia, Berry,
and the monkeys,

THANK YOU!!
Ella xx

48

Stories of fairies

Anna Lester

Illustrated by Teri Gower

Designed by Louise Flutter

Contents

Chapter 1
The tooth fairy   51

Chapter 2
The forgetful fairy   66

Chapter 3
Fairy in a flap   83

Chapter 1

The tooth fairy

It was a fantastic day for Crystal. She had passed her final test at the tooth fairy training school.

Now she could turn children's baby teeth into money.

Jet, Crystal's lazy classmate, had failed all her tests. She would never be a tooth fairy.

It's not fair!

As Jet grumbled, the others flew home and prepared for their first trips.

52

That night, Crystal checked that she had everything she needed...

one bag of magic travel dust...

Check!

Check!

one list of children to visit...

Check!

and, most importantly, her wand.

Crystal sprinkled herself with magic dust. The next second, she was in the bedroom of her first customer, Beth Bingly.

Crystal flew up to the bed. Carefully, she lifted a tooth out from under Beth's pillow.

She aimed her wand at Beth's tooth. "*Zapanasha*!" she cried. But instead of a shiny, new coin, she saw…

Every time she aimed her wand, the tooth changed into something – but never a coin.

Crystal burst into tears. "It's all gone wrong," she sobbed.

Her crying woke Beth, who couldn't believe her eyes.

"Are you the tooth fairy?" she whispered in amazement.

"Yes," wept Crystal, "but it's my first night and I'm useless."

Crystal explained how her wand had failed. "Everyone in Fairyland will laugh at me," she sobbed. "What can I do?"

Beth felt sorry for the fairy. "Let me go back with you," she said. "Maybe I can help."

"Thank you," Crystal sniffed.

A sprinkle of travel dust later, Beth was in Fairyland. The magic powder had made her fairy-sized. She could fly too!

My wand came from the Fantastic Fairy Store.

Then we'll start there.

Beth gasped as she entered
the shop. The walls were lined
with hundreds of fairy outfits.

There were sparkly tiaras,
silky bows, shiny shoes and pots
and pots of gleaming wands.

"How can I help you?" asked
the shopkeeper.

Crystal explained and the
shopkeeper examined the wand.

"This is Jet's wand," she said.
"It will never work properly,
because she's such a bad fairy."

"That sneaky fairy has
swapped her wand for mine,"
cried Crystal.

"Let's get it back," said Beth.

Jet was lazing on the terrace of her tree house. She'd used Crystal's wand to magic up a huge pile of cream cakes.

This is the life.

She was just about to gulp down her tenth eclair, when Crystal and Beth arrived. "Hand over my wand, you thief!" demanded Crystal.

61

"No way, Miss Perfect," said Jet. A stream of stars shot from the wand in her hand. The magical blast turned Crystal's feet to stone.

Can't catch me!

Jet raised the wand to strike again. But suddenly it was snatched from her grasp.

"I'll take that," cried Beth, from a branch above Jet's head.

Jet tried to fly up and grab the wand back. But she'd eaten so much, she couldn't get off the ground.

A second blast from the wand lifted the stony spell from Crystal's feet. She fluttered up to join Beth. "So long, Jet!" cried Crystal as they flew away.

The pair returned to the Fantastic Fairy Store. Crystal bought Beth her very own fairy outfit to thank her.

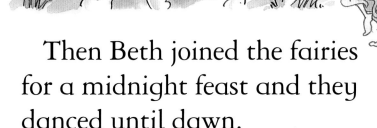

Then Beth joined the fairies for a midnight feast and they danced until dawn.

"Time to say goodbye," said Crystal, showering Beth in magic dust.

In a flash, Beth was back in bed. "What an amazing dream," she thought.

Beth peeked under her pillow. She expected to see her tooth, or even a coin. But what she saw was the tiniest dress in the world.

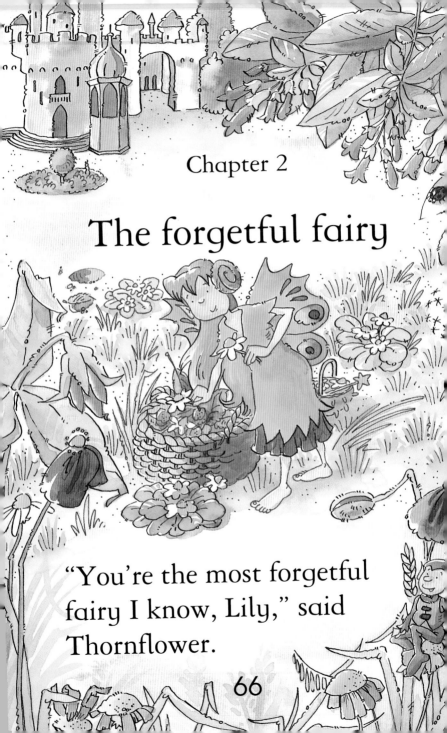

Chapter 2

The forgetful fairy

"You're the most forgetful fairy I know, Lily," said Thornflower.

66

"Since the Fairy Queen's been away, you haven't watered the flowers *or* watched the gnomes. Look at the mess they've made."

"It's time *I* became the Fairy Palace Manager."

"I'm going to make it up to the Fairy Queen," said Lily. "I'm going to organize the best Fairy Ball *ever*."

"Let's hope so," said the Fairy Queen, coming up behind them.

Lily worked
hard all week.
She organized the
Fairy Band.

Bzzzz

Bzzzz

Bzzzz

"Well done, Lily," said the
Fairy Queen.

Thornflower was furious.
"At this rate, I'll never get
her job," she thought angrily.

"Here are the invitations,"
the Fairy Queen added.
"Don't forget, *anyone* with an
invitation can come, so only
give them to guests on the list."

Lily put the invitations in her basket and Thornflower's face lit up in a huge smile.

The hole's still there!

Lily flew all over Fairyland. She visited the Rainbow Fairies and the Garden Fairies.

73

She even flew over the Wild
Woods, to reach the elves and
pixies by the Sunset Sea.

It was only when
Lily got home that
she saw the hole in
her basket.

"Oh no!" she sobbed.
"I forgot to patch it
up. Some of the
invitations might
have dropped out...
and *anyone* could
have found one!"

On the night of the Fairy Ball, Lily stood nervously by the Fairy Queen, watching her welcome each of the guests.

"Well done, Lily," said the Queen. "For once, I don't think you've forgotten a thing."

Just then, the ground began
to shake.

"What can that be?" said the
Fairy Queen. Then she gasped.

An enormous, evil-looking
troll was walking up the hill
to the Fairy Palace.

Lily turned white.

"Don't worry," said the Fairy Queen. "I've cast a spell. Only guests with invitations can come into the palace tonight."

"The trouble is..." Lily began, "I think that troll might *have* an invitation."

78

He did. There was a loud
crash and the troll stuck
his huge, green head
straight through
the palace door.

"Help!" cried the Fairy
Queen. "He'll eat us alive."
"This is all your fault, Lily,"
said Thornflower, gleefully.

79

But the next moment, there was a loud bang followed by a horrible smell. The troll had vanished. In his place stood a Fairy Prince.

"At last!" he cried. "A wicked fairy turned me into a troll. Only coming to a fairy ball could set me free."

"When I found an invitation in the Wild Woods, I was overjoyed."

"I'm so sorry," Lily said to the Fairy Queen. "It was that hole in my basket..."

The Fairy Queen looked thoughtful.

"Never mind, Lily," she said. "The Ball is perfect. And," she added, "it's not every fairy who can turn a troll into a prince."

Chapter 3

Fairy in a flap

Poppy was almost a perfect fairy. Her wand twinkled, her wings shone and her spells never went wrong.

But Poppy
had a problem...

...she couldn't fly.

At school, her friends soared into the sky. Poppy couldn't get off the ground.

"Just keep trying," said the teacher. Poppy flapped her wings until they hurt, but she didn't even hover.

Her mother took her to the
fairy doctor.

"Hmm..." he said. "Stretch
out like a butterfly."

Poppy's wings fluttered open.

And flap...

"She seems fine," he said,
"but try this potion." And he
mixed honey with fluffy clouds.

The potion was delicious,
but it didn't help Poppy fly.
"How do you do it?" she
asked her best friend, Daisy.
Daisy shrugged. "It just
happens," she said.

While her friends did aerobatics, Poppy was stuck in the baby class. As she flapped her wings, a tear rolled down her cheek.

Just then, an imp went past. "What a big baby," he jeered.

Poppy ran from the class
sobbing. She didn't stop until
she reached the forest. Still
crying, she hid in a hollow tree.

"Whooo's that?" hooted an
owl grumpily. "Why the fuss?"

Hiccuping, Poppy told him.
"Imps are so rude," tutted
the owl. "As for learning to fly,
I can teach you. I've taught
hundreds of fledglings."

90

"Jump off a low branch," he ordered, "and flap your wings."

Concentrating hard, Poppy jumped, flapped... and dropped straight to the ground.

"Oooh dear," the owl hooted. "You're thinking about it too much. Never mind. We'll try again tomorrow."

Back at home, Poppy
was making a bandage
from blackberry leaves
when Daisy burst in.

I've found a
spell to make
you fly!

Before Poppy could stop her,
Daisy had waved her wand
and gabbled a spell.

Leave the ground and touch the sky...
Voll-ah-ray Poppy you will fly!

"I feel the same," Poppy said,
doubtfully.

"Try it!" urged Daisy,
pushing her through the door.
"I won't watch."

Poppy took a deep breath
and opened her wings.
Suddenly, she heard a cry.
One of the baby fairies
was stuck high up
in a sunflower.

"Hold on!"
she called and
flew up to the
frightened baby.

As she fluttered back down,
Daisy raced out. "Poppy,
wait. I got the spell wrong..."
She stopped. "Poppy?"

"Yes," said Poppy, with a
big grin. "I can fly!"

With thanks to Russell Punter, Susanna Davidson and Lesley Sims

First published in 2007 by Usborne Publishing Ltd., Usborne House, 83-85 Saffron Hill, London EC1N 8RT, England. www.usborne.com
Copyright © 2007, 2006 Usborne Publishing Ltd.

96